Hello!
We're the Care Bears

We're a special group of colorful, round, snuggly little bears whose job it is to help you understand your own feelings and share them with others.

As you can see, we have special pictures on our tummies, and those pictures tell you the special job each of us loves to do.

I'm Tenderheart Bear, and it's my job to help people reach out to each other. I say that love is a warm, fuzzy feeling, so go ahead and share it.

I'm Cheer Bear, and if you're sad or not feeling well, I'll slide down a rainbow and make you feel better.

Smile! I'm Funshine Bear, so there's a great, big, happy sun on my tummy to remind you to laugh and look at the lighter side of things.

You're in luck 'cause it's me, Good Luck Bear. That's why I'm wearing a four-leaf clover.

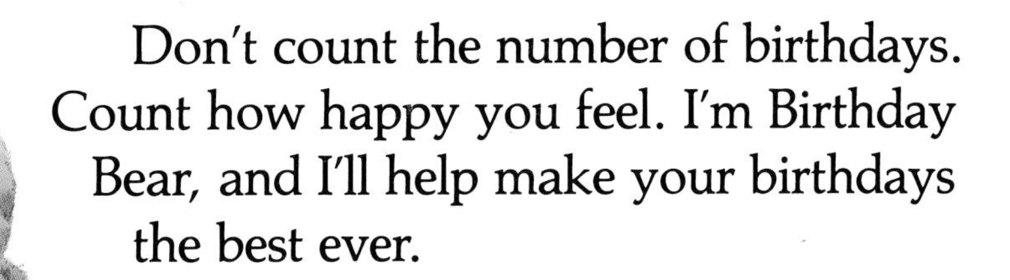

Don't count the number of birthdays. Count how happy you feel. I'm Birthday Bear, and I'll help make your birthdays the best ever.

I'm Wish Bear, and if you wish on my star, maybe your special dream will come true.

If you're ever feeling lonely, just call on me, Friend Bear. See, I've got a daisy for you and a daisy for me.

Grr! I'm Grumpy Bear. There's a cloud on my tummy to show that I take the grouchies away, so you can be happy again.

I'm Love-a-Lot Bear. I have two hearts on my tummy. One is for you; the other is for someone you love.

It's my job to bring you sweet dreams. I'm Bedtime Bear, and right now I'm a bit sleepy. Are you sleepy, too?

Now that you know all of us, we hope that you'll have a special place for us in your heart, just like we do for you.

With love from all of us,

The Care Bears

Published in the United States by Parker Brothers, Division of CPG Products Corp.

Library of Congress Cataloging in Publication Data: Murad, Maria B. The magic words. A Tale from the Care Bears. SUMMARY: When Carrie quarrels with her best friend, the Care Bears help her find the magic words that will mend the friendship.
[1. Friendship—Fiction. 2. Behavior—Fiction. 3. Bears—Fiction] I. Title II. Series.
PZ7.M936Mag 1984 [E] 83-23706 ISBN 0-910313-17-2
Manufactured in the United States of America 4 5 6 7 8 9 0

A Tale from the

Care Bears

The Magic Words

Story by Maria B. Murad
Pictures by Dick Morgado

CHILDRENS PRESS CHOICE
A Parker Brothers title selected for educational distribution
ISBN 0-516-09010-0

For as long as Carrie could remember, she and P.J. had been friends. Every morning, when the sun sparkled through her window, and even when the rain trickled down it, the first thing Carrie saw when she looked out her bedroom window was P.J.'s house next door. His bedroom window was opposite hers, and they waved at each other when they looked out at the same time.

P.J. was Carrie's very best friend, but sometimes one of them would get huffy or mean, and then they would quarrel. Just last week, she and P.J. had planned a picnic, making lemonade and peanut butter and honey sandwiches. But when it was time to eat, they each wanted a different picnic spot. Carrie wanted to eat under the shade tree where her daddy had hung her swing. P.J. wanted to eat in his backyard tent. So they quarrelled, and their good time turned into a sour time.

But today, Carrie was sure they wouldn't fight. Yesterday, P.J. had gotten a beautiful, shiny, red bike for his birthday. It was a two-wheeler with no training wheels. Carrie hurried into her clothes and rushed through her breakfast so she could run next door to try out the new bicycle.

"Take your time, Carrie," said her mother. "P.J.'s bike won't ride away by itself."

"I know," Carrie said, "but P.J. told me to come over early."

She finished her cereal and toast and milk quickly and went out, slamming the kitchen door behind her.

Carrie pushed her way through the bushes between her yard and P.J.'s, anxious to get to the new bike. P.J. had promised her the first ride this morning.

When Carrie got nearer, she could hear a lot of noise. She saw a crowd of children with P.J. and his bicycle, which had white racing stripes and brakes right in the handlebars.

Carrie also saw that someone else was sitting on the bike, and that made Carrie angry. She elbowed her way through the crowd of excited children, straight to P.J.

"P.J.," she said. "You promised *me* the first ride."

P.J. turned and saw Carrie, her hands clenched on her hips.

"Well, sure," he said; "but you weren't here, so I let these kids go first."

"P.J.!" Carrie said. "I thought we were best friends!" She glared at him. "But you're not my friend at all."

Now it was P.J.'s turn to get mad.

"Listen, Carrie," he said, "this is my bike. Wait your turn!"

Carrie's lip was twitching and her nose itched, just like it did when she was going to cry.

"It's an ugly bike, you dumb old P.J.!" she yelled.

"You dumb Carrie!" P.J. yelled back. "Get out of my yard!"

Carrie stared at P.J., and then she ran through the hedge into her own backyard. She could feel tears stinging her eyes.

Her mother was standing outside.

"Oh, Carrie," she said sadly. "I could hear you and P.J. all the way over here. You two can't seem to play without squabbling."

Carrie hung her head. She really did feel like crying.

"Well," said Carrie's mother, "I think it would be better if you didn't go over to P.J.'s house for awhile."

She saw Carrie's sad little face, and she sat down to talk with her.

"Now, Carrie," she said, "you think about it. Remember how you fought over your picnic?"

Carrie's mother sighed and patted her hand.

"Why don't you see if someone else wants to play today?" she suggested. "It's such a lovely day."

Then she went back into the house.

"Huh," Carrie said out loud. "It's not a lovely day anymore."

She even thought she heard a faint rumbling of thunder, but when she looked up at the sky it was as clear and sunny as when she first got up.

Carrie wandered out to her favorite spot under the shade tree, feeling lonely.

"I wish, I wish I knew why P.J. and I fight so much," she said to herself.

"Ahem!" said a deep voice.

Carrie looked up in surprise. A small, furry bear was sitting on her swing. He held a little red umbrella and there was a rain cloud on his tummy.

"Who are you?" asked Carrie.

"I'm Grumpy Bear. I thought I heard a commotion over there," he said, pointing to P.J.'s yard with his umbrella. "And then my tummy started rumbling, so I knew there was trouble. I think maybe I can help you and your friend."

"Oh, really, Grumpy Bear?" asked Carrie. "I hope you can. P.J. and I *are* friends, but we fight a lot. I don't know what to do about it. It just starts somehow, and we end up mad at each other."

Grumpy Bear settled himself nicely on the swing, moving back and forth gently.

"You know, Carrie," he said, "people get into squabbles for lots of reasons. Sometimes different things make us feel mean or out of sorts, and then we quarrel—even with best friends. Often, it's just thoughtlessness."

Carrie thought that over.

"Yes," she said, "I know what you mean. Like when P.J. forgot I had asked to have the first ride."

Grumpy Bear nodded.

"Yes, Carrie," he said, "and you didn't stop to think either. If you had reminded P.J. gently, he probably would have given you the longest ride."

"I never thought of that," Carrie said.

"You see," Grumpy Bear said, "if people really like each other, they'll forgive each other. I've got to go back to Care-a-Lot now, but I have a friend who will be able to help you make up with P.J."

"Oh, Grumpy Bear," Carrie said, "can I meet her?"

"Of course," Grumpy Bear said. "Her name is Love-a-Lot Bear, and she can't stand to see people unhappy. You'll see—she'll fix everything for you and P.J."

Before Carrie could say another word, Grumpy Bear was gone, and she was alone.

Carrie could still hear the laughter from next door. It made her feel sad all over again.

She went slowly inside and up to her room. She sat on her bed and started to cry. She felt that nothing would ever make her friends with P.J. again.

Carrie felt a light touch on her arm. A soft voice said, "Hello."

Carrie saw a chubby little bear with two red hearts on her tummy.

"You must be Grumpy Bear's friend," Carrie said.

The little bear had a wide, sweet smile.

"Yes," she said, "I'm Love-a-Lot Bear. Grumpy Bear told me that you and your friend P.J. are having troubles, so I came to help."

As Carrie watched, the bear bounced off the bed and danced over to the window.

"I see P.J. out there with his bike," Love-a-Lot Bear said. "He looks as lonely as you do."

When Carrie looked out the window she could see P.J. standing by his bike, digging one shoe into the grass. The others were gone.

"Well," Love-a-Lot Bear said briskly, "we can't have all this unhappiness. You see, Carrie," she said softly, "sometimes people who really and truly like each other very much don't take the time to understand each other. You know, you have to be just as polite to your friends as you are to strangers."

"Why," said Carrie, "I think that's the way it is with P.J. and me."

Love-a-Lot Bear nodded wisely.

"Sometimes, we get careless with friends, and forget to treat them as we would like to be treated," she said.

She took Carrie's hands in her little paws.

"I know some magic words, Carrie," she said. "When you forget to be loving and kind, you say these words and everything comes out all right."

Carrie looked at Love-a-Lot Bear. She wanted to believe her, but it seemed almost too good to be true.

Love-a-Lot Bear leaned over and whispered something in Carrie's ear.

Carrie's eyes widened.

"Is that all, Love-a-Lot Bear?" she asked.

"That's all, Carrie," she replied.

"Well," Carrie said, "why didn't I think of that?"

Love-a-Lot Bear just smiled. She touched the hearts on her tummy, did a little turn, and was gone, poof! Just like Grumpy Bear.

Carrie couldn't wait to try the magic words. She ran downstairs and out the back door.

She pushed through the bushes, but slowed down as she came into P.J.'s backyard.

P.J. looked up and saw Carrie.

"P.J.," Carrie said, "You have a beautiful new bicycle, and . . . I'm sorry I yelled at you this morning."

P.J. smiled, a great big smile.

"I'm sorry, too, Carrie," he said. "I didn't stop to remember. I *did* promise you the first ride."

Carrie felt a warm glow. Those little words Love-a-Lot Bear had taught her were really working. "I'M SORRY" *were* truly magic words.

"Carrie," P.J. said, "let's be friends forever and never fight again."

"OK, P.J.," Carrie said. "But maybe if we do squabble, we'll remember the magic words and everything will be all right."

P.J. helped Carrie get on his shiny new bike. He gave her a push, and off she rode, laughing in the sunlight.